20 19 18 17 16 15   1 2 3 4 5 6

LIBRARY OF CONGRESS CATALOGING-IN-PUBLICATION DATA

Tireman, L. S. (Loyd Spencer), 1896–1959, author.
  Quills / stories by Loyd Tireman ; adapted by Evelyn Yrisarri ; layout
and illustrations by Ralph Douglass.
    pages cm — (Mesaland Series ; Book 6)
  "A facsimile of the 1948 first edition."
  Summary: "Follows the adventures of Quills, a funny, lazy porcupine
who stumbles into fresh trouble every minute"— Provided by
publisher.
  ISBN 978-0-8263-5609-3 (cloth : alk. paper) [1. Porcupines—Fiction.
2. Desert animals—Fiction.] I. Yrisarri, Evelyn, adaptor. II. Douglass,
Ralph, illustrator. III. Title.
  PZ7.T5167Qu 2015
  [E]—dc23
                              2015007713

Enemies

Quills, the porcupine, is a strange little animal. He is a great fellow to mind his own business; and he expects others to do the same. He isn't a big animal, nor is he swift. He doesn't have paws with huge claws to tear his enemies. He doesn't have a strong perfume like O'Dor, the skunk. But he does have some-

thing that no other animal has. His back and his flat tail are covered with sharp needle-like quills. They are hidden beneath his thick, coarse hair.

One October morning Quills was walking leisurely over the mesa. His light-tipped, coarse black coat glistened in the sun. He may have been looking for a tender thorn bush. Or perhaps he was headed for the young piñon trees on Mount Baldy. Because he was such a dull and quiet beast, nobody ever knew for sure what he would do next! As he wandered aimlessly along, he heard a little noise ahead of him. It sounded like "pit-pat, pit-pat." Quills never ran away from an enemy. But he took no chances either. Without waiting to see whether the noise was a friend or an enemy, he squatted close to the ground. He tucked his tender nose, his most vulnerable spot, down between his front paws. Every quill on his back stood up. He held his flat tail ready to slap anyone who came too close. He looked like an old-fashioned pin cushion full of pins.

"Pit-pat, pit-pat" — the sound came closer.
Quills sat very still. Then he heard a "sniff,

sniff, sniff." Right away he knew who it was. "Hum, a nice breakfast." Peeping between his paws he saw Three Toes, the coyote. "Hum, hum! What a nice breakfast," said Three Toes, very carefully circling around the porcupine. He took great care, however, to stay out of reach of that threatening tail. The coyote sat down. "Well," he muttered to himself, "I'll just sit here and wait." All was quiet. A fly buzzed past his head. A bird chirped in the juniper tree. The smart old coyote continued, "Maybe that stupid porcupine will think I have gone. I'll wait until he puts down that wicked tail. Then I'll grab him."

No Sir! Quills might be stupid, but he wasn't that big a fool. He knew why the coyote was waiting. "Ha! Ha!" chuckled he, "I'm in no hurry! I can stay here all day." So he crouched closer to the ground. The coyote tired first. With a snort of disgust he gave up. He limped away to look elsewhere for his breakfast. He was too old and too wise to bother a porcupine unless he could catch him unawares. Quills chuckled again. He didn't move for a long time. He wanted to be sure that the sly old coyote had really gone away.

Late that afternoon Quills was plodding along the trail. Again he heard a strange noise. This time it was behind him. "Clump, clump,

clump, clump" went the sound. He didn't wait to look around. Quickly he squatted down and tucked his nose into his paws. He held his tail ready for trouble. "Clump, clump, clump" — nearer came the sounds. Then something raced by him. Quills raised his head a little. Away dashed a beautiful deer. "My," thought Quills, "I'm surely glad I don't need to run away from my enemies like that." He raised his head ready to continue his journey. Suddenly, he heard other sounds coming from behind. There were more animals coming! This time they sounded like dogs. Down went his head. Up went his spines.

Peeping carefully between his paws, Quills saw two young coyotes. They were chasing the deer. As they bounded past the porcupine, the younger coyote stopped. "See what I've found," said he, sitting down to rest. "What is it?" "It's a porcupine," answered his companion. "Is it good to eat?" "Yes, but you have to be careful when you touch it." The younger coyote had never seen a porcupine. He went nearer to investigate. Quills thought that "sniff, sniff" was much too close. He slapped at the sniffing sound with his spiny tail. He hit the inquisitive young coyote right on the nose.

"OH, OH, MY NOSE!

He hit me!" howled the youngster. "My nose is full of needles!" Thoughtlessly he struck at Quills with his front paw. That was a mistake! "Oh," he howled in pain, "my paw! It's full of pins!"

"Well, I told you to be careful," said the

older coyote. "You'd better come away before you get more pins stuck into you." The injured coyote sat down. He tried to rub the stinging spines out of his nose. Instead he only pushed them in deeper. He took hold of a spine in his paw. With a jerk of his head he pulled it out. "Ow!" he howled. "That hurts!" "That's because there are little barbs on each spine," said his friend. "They point backward. Those barbs rip the flesh when they are pulled out." The coyote could do nothing for the spines in his jaws. It would be a long time before they would work out. Painful though his injuries were, he was fortunate. If any of those spines had caught in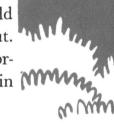

his tongue, he would probably have starved to death.

"Come on," said the older coyote. "You'll learn to leave porcupines alone — if you live long enough." So they trotted away.

Quills listened. He waited until he could hear them no longer. Then he straightened up. Slowly he ambled along the trail toward his burrow in the rocks. It had just been another day to Quills.

Quills

Visits a Ranch

Quills liked to wander over the mesa. He was never, never in a hurry, not even when he was hungry.

On one of his mesa trips he ran into a wire fence. The fence surrounded a ranch house. He tried to crawl under it, but he couldn't.

He tried to climb over it, but he was too clumsy. So he just followed the fence until he came to an open gate.

Going through the opening, he ambled up the path toward the house. It was dusk. At that hour of the day, objects are hard to see. This gave the little porcupine a chance to wander around without being bothered.

Inside the ranch house Mrs. Brown had just finished washing dishes. She opened the door to throw out the water. In the dusk she saw Quills, who had just reached the back porch. "Ker-splash" went the water, nearly drowning the porcupine.

Closing the door she said, "I just threw my dishwater on a funny little animal outside." "Probably a skunk," answered Mr. Brown, "I thought I smelled one when I came in."

Quills was certainly surprised when he was covered with the warm water. It wasn't hot enough to hurt him. He sniffed around. But he didn't find anything to eat.

So he wandered along around the house.
Soon he reached the Brown's woodpile.

"Sniff! sniff! Something smells good," he
thought happily.

He began searching. Soon he found the
smell. It was on an ax handle. The handle

was salty from the sweaty hands of the men who had used it.

Salt is one of the finest treats a porcupine can find. Quills was delighted. He began to gnaw.

While Quills was busy chewing, the ranch cat came around the woodpile. She carried a mouse in her mouth. When she saw the prickly porcupine, she dropped the mouse. She arched her back and began hissing like a steam engine. Quills paid no attention to the cat. He wasn't afraid of her. He continued to munch calmly on the ax handle.

After a while he had eaten all he wanted. He decided to see what else he could find around the place. He ambled along until he came to the barn. "This is a strange place," he thought, "Wonder what's in here?"

Going in, he stumbled upon a leather saddle. Someone had carelessly thrown it on the floor. "Umm, umm," mutters Quills, "This looks good." He sat down to chew the deli-

cious tasting saddle. It probably tasted like chocolate cake would to a little boy.

One of the ranch dogs came past the woodpile and smelled the porcupine. He followed the trail until he found Quills in the barn.

The dog knew how dangerous a porcupine's flat tail could be. He knew enough not to get too close to Quills. From a respectful distance, he began to growl.

"What are you doing here?" he barked, "Get away from those saddles!" Mr. Brown heard the dog.

"Shep must have found the skunk you threw the water on," he said, "I'd better go out and shoot it."

"You'd better not," said Mrs. Brown, "It's dark and the skunk might spray you. If it did, I'd never get the smell washed out of your clothes." "All right," said Mr. Brown, as he went back to bed. "We'll let the dog take care of Mr. Skunk."

Quills wasn't a bit afraid of Shep. He knew the dog wouldn't come too close. He continued to chew the saddle.

Soon he had eaten all he wanted. He took a short walk around the barnyard. He didn't find anything else to eat, so he left the ranch.

The next morning Mr. Brown went out to the woodpile. He was certainly surprised to find the ruined handle. Later he went into the barn. When he saw the chewed saddle, he was furious. "So that was why the dog was barking last night," he said to himself. "It wasn't a skunk after all. It's my own fault. I can't be too hard on the dog. He barked and barked to warn me. No smart dog would attack a porcupine and get his nose full of spines."

Mr. Brown examined the saddle which Quills had chewed. "Guess I can fix it," he grumbled, "And I'll also fix the next porcupine I find around here."

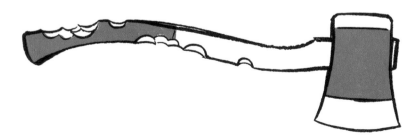

Quills and the Bluejays

Quills, the porcupine, was pattering through a grove of pine trees one morning. He was looking for some nice tender bark to eat. He sat down before a nice-looking, tall young tree.

"This looks like a good one," he said to himself. "Surely, I'll find some nice, tender bark near the top, or even some mistletoe."

Slowly he began to climb. Up, he went past
the first limb. Up, up, past the second. Up,
up, up, past the third and fourth limbs.

As he was nearing the top of the tree, his
head bumped into something. He looked up

slowly. It was a bird's nest. It wasn't very large but it was right in his way. If he climbed any higher, he would have to crawl over it.

"Well, maybe this bark is tender," said Quills. "Perhaps I won't need to go any farther."

He looked at the tree trunk beneath his feet. Then he tore off a piece of the outer bark. He took a bite from the inner bark.

"Ugh! It's tough," he grumbled, "I'll just have to climb higher."

Quills didn't really like the idea of climbing over the nest. He sat down to think.

"I could back down and find another tree, I suppose. But that would take too long. I'm hungry. Guess I'll just have to climb over that nest."

So he put his paws up on the edge. Then he slowly raised his head over the side. That was a mistake, for in that nest lived a family of bluejays.

Mrs. Fussy Bluejay had heard Quills com-

ing up the tree. She thought it might be one of her friends, so she had not been alarmed. But when she saw Quills' black nose poking over the edge of the nest, that was something different! She had a nest full of baby bluejays to protect.

"HELP, HELP!"

she shrieked in her loud, rough voice. "Get out of here, you old porcupine!"

Poor, slow, dull-witted Quills! He was so surprised and so frightened by the noise! He had no intention of harming anyone.

"All I want," quavered the porcupine, "is to climb over your nest to the top of the tree where the bark is tender."

"You're not going to climb over my babies," screeched Mrs. Fussy, "Help! Get down! Go away!"

Quills was really a kind fellow. He didn't want any trouble with Fussy Bluejay. So with a deep sigh he began to feel for the limb beneath him. This fumbling around was too slow for Fussy Bluejay.

"Go away, I told you!" screamed Fussy, and she pecked sharply at his tender nose.

"Oh, oh, my nose!" groaned Quills. He

was so confused and astonished that he couldn't move.

"Why, I have never before met such an angry bird," he thought.

"Help! help!" shrilled Fussy. She pecked his nose again. She couldn't take any chances with that spiney old animal. He might hurt her babies.

From far away, Mr. Bluejay had heard Fussy's cry for help. He flew swiftly to his home. There he saw Quills clinging to the tree. Above him was the angry mother bluejay.

"Of all things!" he squawked. "A porcupine trying to climb into our nest! Poor Fussy trying to protect the babies from that horrid animal."

Mr. Bluejay was furious. "I'll teach you to let our nest alone."

Without any more warning, Mr. Bluejay went into action. He whirled upon Quills so fast that the poor little animal didn't know what was happening. Every time Mr. Jay flew by he rapped Quills sharply with his beak.

By now Quills was so bewildered he couldn't think. He couldn't find the limb below. And, also, his nose hurt dreadfully.

Quills did his best to protect himself from the angry bluejays. In his struggles he lost his footing on the limb. Down he fell.

He crashed down through the branches. Down, down, down! He fell past the fourth limb, past the third, and past the second. Then he bounced on the first branch and landed on the ground, "Ker plunk."

Quills lay very still. His breath had been knocked out of him.

Both Mr. and Mrs. Bluejay swooped down, ready to continue their attack. When they

saw their recent enemy lying very still, they began to laugh raucously.

"Aha! that old porcupine won't bother us again!"

"I guess we can protect our babies," shrieked Mr. Jay. And off he flew to tell his neighbors about the porcupine robber. But Quills wasn't dead. The pine branches had helped to break his fall. Also he had landed on his back and his thick cushiony tail had saved him from injury.

First Quills moved one leg, then another, then all four. He rolled over and sat up. Tenderly he felt of his nose.

"Oh me! Oh my! How my nose hurts!" he groaned as he stumbled toward his rocky den. Before going too far, he stopped and looked back very carefully at the tree from which he had fallen.

"I want to be sure to stay away from that tree. I never want to see those dreadful Bluejays again."

The Tree Dweller

The warm autumn days were passing. Chill wintry winds began to blow. The brush and bushes on the mountainside dried up. Food became very scarce for Quills, the little porcupine. This meant that he would have to spend more time in the trees. He didn't care. He found the food at the "tree-top cafe" very good. For breakfast there were nice, tender, double-decker bark sandwiches. Pine needle salad was always on the menu for lunch, with cold slices of pine bark at supper-time. The dessert was especially good: pine gum-drops were always plentiful at the tree café.

For this reason Quills spent a great deal of

his time in the trees during the winter. Since he was so slow and clumsy, he became a tree dweller. That is, he just moved into a tree and stayed. It made life much easier for he didn't have to go up and down every time he was hungry.

This year, Quills chose a little piñon as his winter home. He was the only tenant. That suited him very well as he didn't like company. He liked to be alone.

Being a tree dweller is very exciting. There are so many things to see. And so many things happen. Sometimes Quills would hear the deep musical "honk, honk," of wild geese. Watching, he would see them fly toward the south seeking a warmer climate. Once a black bear lumbered past. Very often, the little winter birds would pause awhile in their swift flight to rest and gossip.

Some days the bright sun would melt the snow a little. But by night the north wind would return and it would be very cold.

Quills never seemed to mind the weather. He was never too hot in the summer nor too cold in the winter.

It was the little birds who noticed the cold weather.

One day in mid-winter a little bird flew up to Quills. Shivering and shaking she said, "The wind is so cold today. May I sit beside you and get warm?"

Quills didn't seem to mind although he did not answer. Sometimes these fluttery birds made him nervous with all their chattering and gossiping.

Quills was really a kind fellow. So he sheltered the little bird from the wind.

Because of Quills' kindness to her the little bird sang a sweet song for him:

"I came to the tree
  cold and weary
I left the tree
  warm and cheery."

One morning as Quills sat chewing a bit of bark, he heard the sound of animals, running. Looking between the branches, he saw a doe, with a fawn close beside her.

"Something must be chasing that deer," he thought.

Just then he saw the mountain lion. Slipping along close behind the doe and fawn, it sniffed their trail. It came nearer to Quills' tree.

Quills froze to his branch. What if the mountain lion noticed him perched in the tree? He was afraid of mountain lions. They killed porcupines. His heart beat fast.

The lion paid no attention to Quills. He knew that a fawn was better eating than a porcupine. So he continued to follow the trail of the doe and the fawn. Quills gave a sigh of relief.

A few days later Quills had another bad scare. He heard a crashing through the underbrush. Peeping out through the branches,

Quills saw the cause of the noise. It was a man. With him were hunting dogs.

"He must be looking for that mountain lion," thought Quills, terrified. "I won't move, and maybe he won't see me."

Quills' spiney needles were standing on end. His back looked almost like the needles on the piñon tree. Perhaps that was the reason the hunter didn't notice the porcupine, for he, too, passed by on the trail of the lion.

One night while Quills was fast asleep with his four legs straddling the branch, the snow came. Softly and quietly the flakes fell. They covered the needles and boughs of the trees like a white, fluffy blanket.

The snow piled high on the branches. They became so heavy that they sank lower and

lower until the porcupine was shut into a little private snow room.

When daylight came, Quills awoke. He was hungry. He moved along the branch toward the end. There he could find some tender needles to eat. As he moved, the snow shifted on the upper branches. Without a sound or warning, "ker-plop!", a big pile of snow fell right on him. He was covered completely.

The snow was heavy. It almost knocked Quills off the branch. His front feet slipped. He hung on with his sharp hind toes. He teetered back and forth on the swaying branch. As he teetered, more snow drifted down from the upper branches. Even his eyes were full.

Up and down, up and down, he went.

"My, oh my! I'm going to fall," he thought.

Finally, with the help of his bristly tail, he was able to balance himself. After he was quietly settled again on the branch, he rubbed the snow out of his eyes. Reproachfully he looked at the upper branches of the piñon tree. "They tried to make me fall," he grumbled to himself. "They pushed snow on me."

The days passed slowly. One day the south wind blew very gently. The weather seemed to be getting warmer.

"It's so warm the buds and leaves must be coming out on the bushes," Quills said to him-

self. "Some fresh buds would taste mighty good."

Carefully he backed down the tree. He hunted everywhere but he couldn't find any fresh leaves. The bushes were still bare.

Winter wasn't over! A few nice warm days do not make Spring. Quills was disappointed. He wanted some tender new buds to eat. He looked around carefully for another tree. This time he would stay. At least he would stay until he was sure that Spring had really arrived.

Quills lived in the tree many weeks. During his stay he ate most of the bark from the top of the tree. It was ruined and would never be as lovely as it was before. But that is the law of Nature.

The Little Yellow Pine Tree

Beyond the mesa, where the foothills swept up to Mt. Baldy, stood a tree. It was a little yellow pine tree.

It stood straight and tall, proud of its strong boughs and green needles. At the foot of the little pine grew beautiful wild flowers. Hovering above her were fluffy white clouds in a sky of azure blue.

Every morning the little tree waited for the first beams of the rising sun. All day she lifted

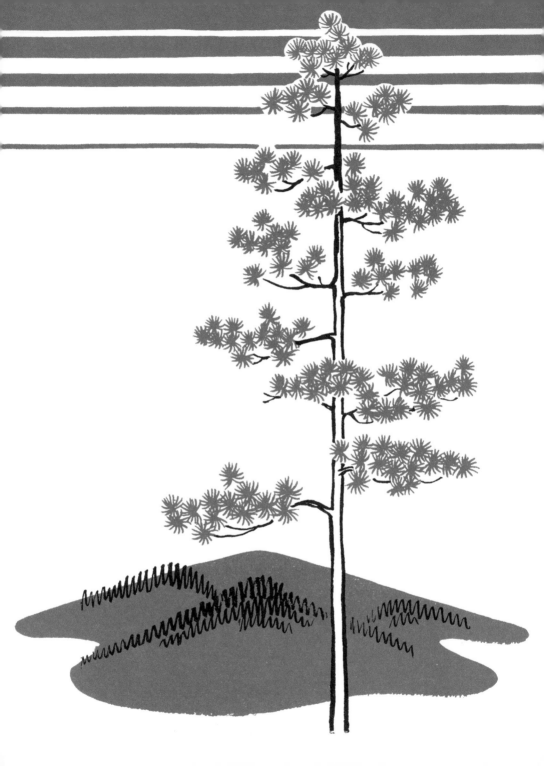

her face to the powerful Sun God. With each passing sunlit hour some of his strength and beauty seemed to enter the little pine. During the long silent hours of the night, the little tree drank in the majesty and peace of the distant stars.

The proud little tree had only one wish. She sang to herself as she swayed in the mountain breezes.

"Oh, that I might grow straight and beautiful like the pines on yonder mountains. Oh, that my top might be slender and tall."

As the years passed, her song and wish were fulfilled. She rose limb by limb into a perfection of slender beauty.

Then one day as she was singing her usual song to the breezes, she was filled with horror and fear. Her beautiful crown might be ruined! Her beauty might be spoiled! Coming out of the forest toward her was a funny-looking little animal. Its light-tipped hair shone in the sunlight. It was covered with spines down the back and along its tail. It was Quills, the porcupine.

Quills made straight for a little fir tree close by. Slowly, slowly, he climbed up to the top and started to eat the tender bark. Before many days the top of the little tree began to die.

Not long after that the little yellow pine again shook with fear. She saw Quills climb another neighboring tree. This time the porcupine ate the buds and the ends of the branches. In a few weeks the branches of that tree turned brown.

Now the little yellow pine tree lived in constant fear.

"What if the porcupine comes to me and tears my bark," she thought. "I could then never, never grow to be beautiful like the pines in the forest."

From that day the little pine ceased to watch

for the first morning sunbeams. Instead, she watched in fear for the little black porcupine. Weeks slowly passed but nothing happened.

Then one morning the little yellow pine shook its needles in horror. All of her fears were coming true! Quills was coming toward her.

Slowly, slowly, Quills climbed the little yellow pine tree. Up, up, up he went to the top branches. Finding a suitable place, he propped himself against the trunk with his tail. Then he began to tear the tender bark with his sharp teeth. "Oh, oh," wailed the pine needles. "Can nothing save us?" "Must my beauty be ruined?" moaned the beautiful tree.

The yellow pine was sunk in despair. What could help her now?

Then far away in the forest, she heard a deep sigh. It was the wind sweeping through the trees. Dark clouds rolled heavily up the sky. Soon thunder roared. Lightning flashed as the storm moved closer.

Huge raindrops came pattering down. Quills paid no attention to the storm. A little rain didn't bother him. He sat and ate peacefully.

The storm became more severe. The lightning ripped the dark sky. The thunder crashed angrily.

Then suddenly there came a terrific blinding flash. A sheet of light brighter than all the other flashes lighted the mountainside. It was so bright that it blinded Quills. He couldn't see what was happening. He lost his balance and fell to the ground.

The fall didn't hurt him. He was used to falling out of trees. The ground was soft from

the rain. But the rain was coming so fast that he could scarcely see.

Quills picked himself up and started toward his rocky den. He would wait there. Then the lightning wouldn't blind him again.

After a while the storm passed.

The little yellow pine tree gave a deep sigh of relief. She was deeply grateful to the storm. It had come in time to help her. She was saved from ruin. She shook the rain from her needles, raised her limbs, and swaying in the breeze began to sing:

"Once more I'm free! I'll grow straight and tall and beautiful like the pines on yonder mountains."

The end

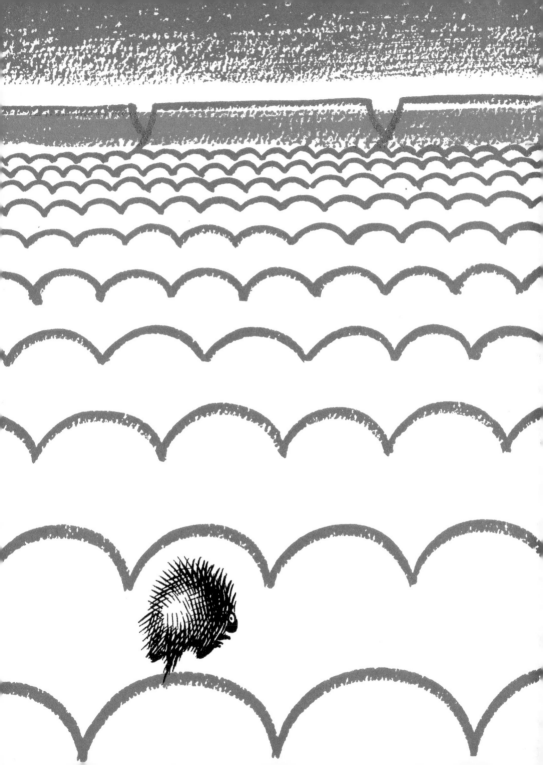